MAMA LIKES TO MAMBO

HELAINE BECKER • JOHN BEDER

Stoddart
Kids
TORONTO • NEW YORK

Published in Canada in 2001 by
Stoddart Kids,
a division of Stoddart Publishing Co. Limited
895 Don Mills Road, 400-2 Park Centre
Toronto, Canada M3C 1W3
Tel (416) 445-3333 Fax (416) 445-5967
E-mail cservice@genpub.com

Distributed in Canada by
General Distribution Services
325 Humber College Blvd.
Toronto, Canada M9W 7C3
Tel (416) 213-1919 Fax (416) 213-1917
E-mail cservice@genpub.com

Published in the United States in 2002 by
Stoddart Kids,
a division of Stoddart Publishing Co. Limited
180 Varick Street, 9th Floor
New York, New York 10014
Toll free 1-800-805-1083
E-mail gdsinc@genpub.com

Distributed in the United States by
General Distribution Services, PMB 128
4500 Witmer Industrial Estates
Niagara Falls, New York 14305-1386
Toll free 1-800-805-1083
E-mail gdsinc@genpub.com

05 04 03 02 01 1 2 3 4 5

Canadian Cataloguing in Publication Data

Becker, Helaine, 1961–
Mama likes to mambo

ISBN 0-7737-3316-7

1. Children's poetry, Canadian (English).* I. Beder, John. II. Title.

PS8553.E295532M35 2001   jC811'.6   C2001-930585-0
PR9199.4.B42M35 2001

THE CANADA COUNCIL | LE CONSEIL DES ARTS
FOR THE ARTS | DU CANADA
SINCE 1957 | DEPUIS 1957

*We acknowledge for their financial support of our
publishing program the Canada Council, the Ontario Arts
Council, and the Government of Canada through the
Book Publishing Industry Development Program (BPIDP).*

Printed and bound in Hong Kong, China
by Book Art Inc., Toronto

For Karl, Michael and Andrew.
— H.B.

For Carolyn and Alex.
— J.B.

Mama Likes to Mambo

Mama likes to mambo
Daddy likes to swing
Baby Ray likes reggae
'Cuz wailing is her thing

And we all love to dance
Whenever there's a chance

So jump up, shakalaka
Jump up, shakalaka
Shake your body, shakalaka
If you love to dance!

Simon likes salsa
I think jazz is neat
Little Hank goes gaga
For that racy raga beat

Since we ALL love to dance
Whenever there's a chance

Let's boogie down, rambalam
Boogie down, rambalam
Really jam, rambalam
If you love to dance!

Be-bop and hip hop
Rock and roll and the stroll
Funk and blues and R&B
Why not cha-cha-cha with me?

When you can, shake it, shake it
Don't be shy, don't try to fake it
Just be careful not to break it!

C'mon now, let's D-A-N-C-E!

Down by the Bay

The slip-slap, slip-slap slop of a flip-flop
Sings the song of summer
Down by the bay

Hot rocks, bleached docks, sandy toes with no socks
Stir the soul of summer
Down by the bay

Mudpies, tied flies, listening for loon cries
I can't wait for summer
Down by the bay.

Popsicle

Do be careful how you eat it
Do not slurp it or mistreat it
Do not lick it super-slow
Or try and gulp it in one go
Do not nibble up one side
Or ignore it while you stride
It will end up on the ground
Sunshine lost, and sorrow found
Once, a perfect Popsicle
But now . . . just a

d
  r
    o
      p
        s
          i
            c
              l
                e

The Carpenter's Ball

Have you been to the Carpenter's Ball?
It's the greatest bash of them all
They pound with hammers to keep the beat
Then do the jig with saws on their feet
And when they get tired, they make their own seats
At the Colossal Carpenter's Ball.

Have you been to the Farmer's Ball?
They raise the roof from summer to fall
They polka with pigs for the first dance
Then offer the chickens their own cha-cha chance
The scarecrow emcees by the seat of his pants
At the Fantastic Farmer's Ball.

Have you been to the Teacher's Ball?
It's held every week in Study Hall
The teachers compete to Tango the best
Then whip out red pens for marking the test
And give out detentions to all of the rest
At the Terrific Teacher's Ball.

Have you been to the Fisherman's Ball?
Making a splash is the aim of it all
The ticket price is a fabulous deal
Since you cast out a line and catch your own meal
The favorite dance? The Virginia Reel
At the Frolicsome Fisherman's Ball.

Have you been to the Policeman's Ball?
Where walking the beat is done by all
Jailhouse Rock is the song of the day
The cops chant together, "Crime does not pay!"
And robbers and crooks are taken away
From the Popular Policeman's Ball.

Have you been to the Sailor's Ball?
Where rocking and rolling won't wait for a squall
They hold the party while under sail
They dip with the dolphin, then waltz with the whale
Things really get wild if there's a gale
At the Sensational Sailor's Ball.

Have you been to the Firefighter's Ball?
It really is the hottest ticket of all
Even the DJ starts feeling the heat
When the chiefs get down to the burning backbeat
"Disco Inferno," has 'em out of their seats
At the Fabulous Firefighter's Ball.

Have you been to the Mom's and Dad's Ball?
Admission to it is the strictest of all
They all flash pictures of their perfect kids
And share precious stories of what Junior did
But then lose their tempers and flip their lids
At the Marvelous Mom's and Dad's Ball.

But have you been to the Children's Ball?
This is the one that's the most fun of all
The Teddy Bear band sure knows how to play
There's candy and cake and chocolate all day
And none of the parents dare disobey
So come to the Children's Ball!

Sparkle the Spaniel

There once was a spaniel named Sparkle
Who had an inferior barkle
He sought and got help
For his pitiful yelp
And now he's top dog at the parkle.

A Jolly
Jurassic Christmas

At Christmastime, in days of yore
'Twas great to be a dinosaur
The Duckbills jingled all the way
Pulling Santa Claus's sleigh

The Longnecks strung up all the lights
The Hadrosaurs had snowball fights
And at the Festive Fossil Bash
Apatosaurus made a splash

Spinosaurus spiked the punch
Then burped and hiccuped all through lunch
Giganta gorged on gingerbread
Got scolded and was sent to bed

The Stego-chorus sounded swell
When it sang "Noel, Noel"
But as the carolers came to greet him
T-Rex felt he had to eat them!

The Christmas tree was quite a sight
Once Diplodocus took a bite
The Raptors wrapped the gifts all night
But didn't get the name tags right!

So Allosaur got salad tongs
And CDs full of heartbreak songs
Triceratops got underwear
And whined all day, it wasn't fair!

But all in all, they had a ball
And celebrated 'til Last Call
And now they want to raise a toast
To all the kids they love most

So here's to you, from the Jurassic
We hope your Christmas is fantastic!

Rumble Bumble Bumblebee

I rambled through the bramble with a rumble bumble bee
And this is what that rumble bumble rambler said to me:

Roly poly ram-ba-lam
Jambalaya, toast and jam
Hambone, wishbone, Ping-Pong slam

Rhubarb crumble,
Thank you ma'am!

Tommy Treasure Hunter

Tommy Hunter is my name
And treasure hunting is my game
I don my hiking boots and cap
I grab my compass and a map.

Let's start the expedition then
Down the hall and past the den
Treasure's everywhere, you see
If you're smart and brave like me.

I told you so! Behind that chair!
It's pirate treasure buried there
And those are Spanish gold doubloons
Mixed with all the silver spoons!

Shhhh!

Dare we pinch a dragon's hoard?
It's over there — on Mom's sideboard
And if you'll brave the laundry room
I'll take you to the mummy's tomb.

Yes, hidden treasure's everywhere
And if you find some, *we can share!*

Apple Pandowdy

Apple Pandowdy, my favorite dish
I like it far better than salted codfish
I like to eat mine with gobs of ice cream
And when it's all gone, I lick the bowl clean.

Carmen Miranda

Carmen Miranda wore fruit on her head
She offered two pears to the Lady in Red
The Lady declined
(She'd already dined)
So Carmen Miranda ate them instead.

(No wonder she always looked so well fed!)

The Small Round Poem

A ball, of course
A ladybug
An old and faded braided rug

A daisy's eye
Bright like the sun
Umbrella tops
That make rain fun

A lollipop
My grandma's hat
A curled up, sleeping ginger cat

Cookies on a cookie plate
That look so good, I just can't wait
Coins to buy ice-cream to go
A globe to shake that's full of snow

All these things are quite alike
I'm sure you will agree
They're small and round and wonderful
They're quite a lot like me!

The
Tall
Thin
Poem

Lollipops with rainbow tops
A fire truck's long ladder
A green and purple dangling snake
(What type I'm sure won't matter!)

Palm trees wearing coconuts
Atop their shaggy heads
A pile of peas, for princesses
And royal feather beds

A totem pole, all carved in wood,
Toronto's CN Tower
My grandpa's own grandfather clock
Chiming every hour

Giraffes, of course
Flamingos too, on tip toe in a lake
And candles burning oh-so-bright
On sky-high birthday cake

All these things are quite alike
I'm sure you will agree
They're tall and thin and wonderful
They're quite a lot like me!

Wallace P. "Wiggy" Wigden

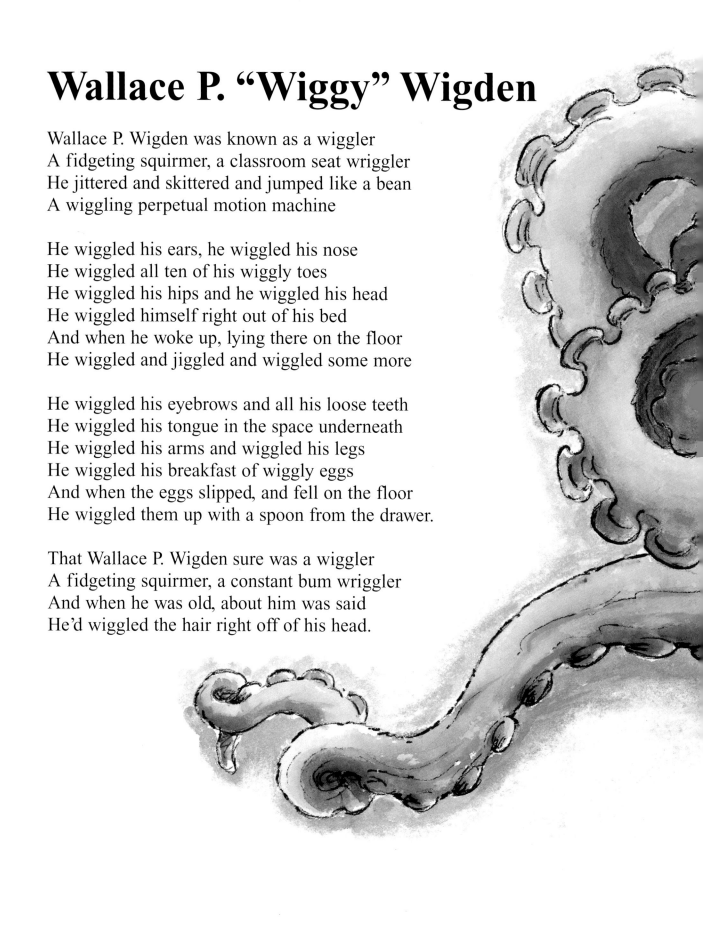

Wallace P. Wigden was known as a wiggler
A fidgeting squirmer, a classroom seat wriggler
He jittered and skittered and jumped like a bean
A wiggling perpetual motion machine

He wiggled his ears, he wiggled his nose
He wiggled all ten of his wiggly toes
He wiggled his hips and he wiggled his head
He wiggled himself right out of his bed
And when he woke up, lying there on the floor
He wiggled and jiggled and wiggled some more

He wiggled his eyebrows and all his loose teeth
He wiggled his tongue in the space underneath
He wiggled his arms and wiggled his legs
He wiggled his breakfast of wiggly eggs
And when the eggs slipped, and fell on the floor
He wiggled them up with a spoon from the drawer.

That Wallace P. Wigden sure was a wiggler
A fidgeting squirmer, a constant bum wriggler
And when he was old, about him was said
He'd wiggled the hair right off of his head.

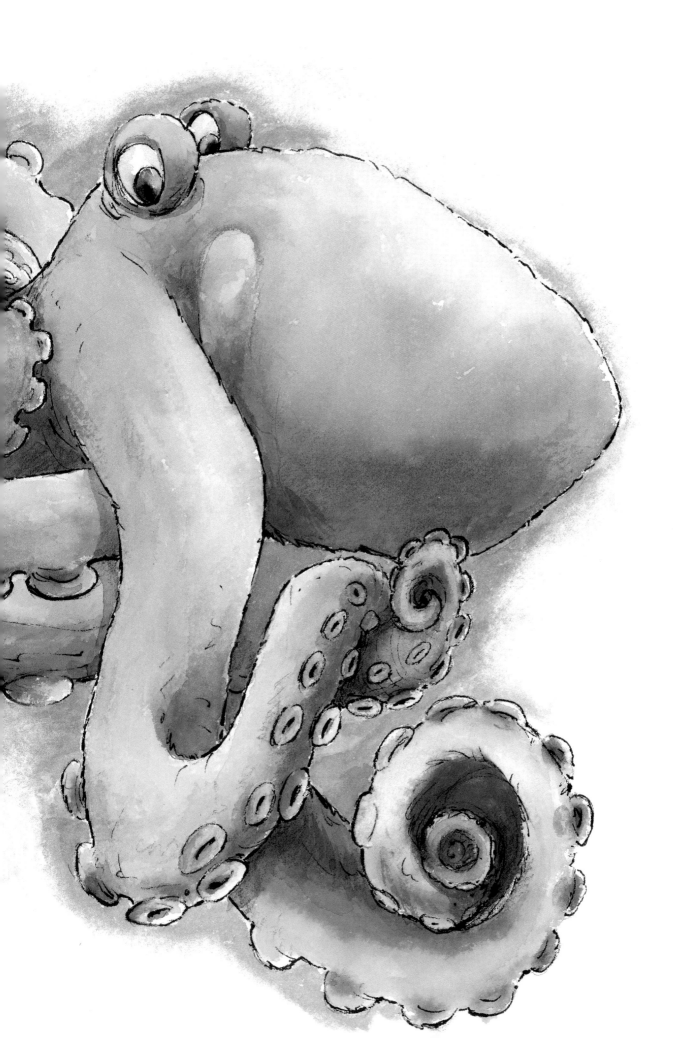

Hurricane Hissy

I have a little sister
She's as sweet as she can be
She's quick to share her teddy bear
And other toys with me.

But Melissa has a temper
As Mom is wont to say
And when Missy throws a hissy fit
You best stay far away.

Her eyes roll up, her fists they clench
Her lips turn vivid blue
The shrieks she makes are like a knife
They cut you right in two.

One day my mom asked Missy
To go pick up her clothes
I saw a temper tantrum
Start forming near her toes.

I dove behind the sofa
With not a breath to spare
Before my mom could stop her
She was stomping on a chair.

Her golden curls were shaking with
The rage built up inside
There was an awful quaking
As she ranted, raved and cried.

The air grew faintly purple
And sparks began to fly
A scorching bolt of lightning
Jumped from Missy to the sky.

She whirled around and shook her fists
A dervish on a tear
Then a tantrum-spawned tornado
Sprang loose from Missy's hair.

It slammed across the kitchen
Leaving chaos in its wake
It burst the pipes and soon
We all were standing in a lake.

The storm swept through the playroom
And out the sliding door
It gathered speed on Main Street
With a truly frightening roar.

Busses crashed, roofs tore loose
The rains came in a rush
Transport trucks were overturned
A hot dog cart was crushed.

But still the tantrum did not stop
My sis was on a roll
She stamped her feet upon the floor
Until they'd made a hole.

The hole grew deep, and deeper still
I stared at it with wonder
I just had time to leap before
The house fell *in*, by thunder!

I felt a rumble down below
The ground began to shake
Missy's temper tantrum
Was now a huge earthquake!

Sirens blared an awful shriek
Alarms rang loud and clear
The weather girl soon announced
A hurricane was here.

They called it Hurricane Hissy
And charted out its course
It hovered overhead awhile
Then headed south with force.

It soon crossed Lake Ontario
And you can do the math
New York's ports and Philly
Were directly in its path

But even worse the quake had caused
A tidal wave to form
The Great Lakes (gulp!) were rising
Far higher than the norm.

A towering Tsunami completely
Flattened Buffalo
And Cleveland and Detroit
Were the next big burgs to go.

Yet still Melissa carried on
A global-scale disaster
When Florida slid in the drink
The winds whipped even faster.

They blew Bermuda off the map
Into the stratosphere
Brazil's another planet now
Six zillion miles from here.

The Swiss Alps are a valley
The Gobi is a lake
The Pyramids are upside down —
Egyptian wedding cake.

Let's not forget Los Angeles
Is drifting out to sea
And Calgary and Edmonton
Are beachfront property!

But at last my sis began to tire
Her lip began to quiver
She slumped and curled up in a ball
And tried hard not to shiver.

While rescue crews began their work
My mom got busy too
She picked up little Missy
Knowing just what she should do.

Mom covered her with kisses
And softly stroked her hair
She held her tight and rocked her then
In Grandma's rocking chair.

Outside the world had blown apart
Ripped open at the seams
But we were safe and sound with Mom
Wrapped up in hugs and dreams.

And so the little whirlwind
Sighed contentedly and deep
That hissy fit had done its bit
And Missy was asleep.

Yes, I have a little sister
She's as sweet as she can be
But if she has a hissy fit
You'd better hide with me!

Who Stole the Baby?

I used to have a baby
As cute as cute could be
That cuddly little cherub
Used to live right here with me.

He played with a stuffed bunny
And slept within a crib
I would feed him in a highchair
As he dribbled on his bib.

But someone stole the baby
When I looked the other way
And swapped him for the big boy
That just showed up one day.

He's quite a charming child
All legs and arms and grins
He has a lot of big kid toys
He keeps in colored bins.

He's crazy about dinos
And loves to count the stars
He builds elaborate towers
And crashes Hot Wheel cars.

I'm glad to have this big boy
He really is a treat
But still I miss my baby
And his chubby little feet.

I think about that infant coo
And precious toothless grin
But then the boisterous big boy
Shouts, "Come on and tuck me in."

And he looks so sweet and sleepy
All cuddled up in bed
As I bend down to kiss him
On the top of his sweet head.

I wonder how I managed
Before I knew this boy
But Bunny's there beside him
My baby's favorite toy.

I start to sing quite softly
An old familiar air
And the big boy faintly smiles
As I stroke his thick, short hair.

Yes someone stole the baby
And I miss him, it is true
But I would never take back baby
If it meant that I'd lose you.

Sleepwalker's Dilemma

I woke up in a muddle
In the middle of a puddle
Had the poodle made a piddle in the middle
Of the night?

Was the puddle poodle piddle
Or had I leaked a little
And made a piddle of my own, was the riddle
Of the night.

Did I dare to take a peek
To see who took a leak
By switching on my light in the middle
Of the night?

Hoorah! It wasn't piddle
Only water spilled a little
And the piddle riddle petered out that
Puddle muddle night.